Christmas with the Rural Mail

A poem
by LANCE WOOLAVER
to accompany paintings
and hand painted Christmas cards
by MAUD LEWIS

NIMBUS
PUBLISHING
LIMITED

In the mail a Box was sent,
Full of Toys, by sleigh it went,
Through the country by the Bay,
For the Baby's Christmas Day.

Up the hillside sped the Mail,
Past the Bay and Fish for Sale,
Ships ashore and boats turned over,
And bluebirds' houses all snowed under.

Down they came from Digby Ridge,
Sleighbells rang in the covered bridge,
Children sliding on the frozen river
Made the pony shake and shiver.
A small boy heard the sleighbells' noise
And hoped the mailsleigh carried toys.

The pony stopped to share a joke
With oxen shackled to the yoke.
They told him that they'd like to be
Allowed to run about and free.

But two brown Clydesdales down the road
Were proud to haul a heavy load.
They're Champions at the Weymouth Fair:
Most Weight Pulled by a Heavy Pair.

The pony shook his bells. Good-bye!
The oxen blinked their eyes and sighed.
The horse team snaked the spruce logs down
To the mill by the stream that runs through town.

Bluebirds, digging out their nest,
Thought they might like summer best.
After one last song they planned
To wing for Christmas in a warmer land.

Buntings, nestling in the snow,
Where the partridge berries grow,
Listened as the whispering breeze
Played tunes on the icicles in the trees.
Startled, when the pony sifted by,
Lifted up to the clear blue sky.

A black horse, out to get some sun,
Showed the pony who could run.
His driver tried to stop the sleigh
But the bad horse upped and ran away.

The mailsleigh waited for the steaming train.
Passengers patted the pony's mane.
Two old sisters, arm in arm,
Walked from the Station to their father's farm.
HELLO they called, to the Christmas sleigh,
We're home again for Christmas Day.

As they passed Acaciaville,
Children playing on Ben's Hill,
Hailed the driver, laughed and cried,
And waved to the pony as the sleigh sped by.

The pony stopped by a Rural Box,
The driver bent his head to talk
With Little Pearl, all hat and grin,
Came out to bring the presents in.
Last stop! The pony turned the sleigh,
Home to the barn and summer hay.

Two white-tailed deer, at the close of day,
Walked to the Town along the Bay,
Saw the Christmas presents come,
Wished the pony brought them some.

Christmas Eve and through the Night,
Snowbanks gleamed in the bright moonlight,
Over the ice the North Wind blew,
Under the ice Belle River flew.
The pony slept. The Night was wild.
He dreamed of the toys he'd brought to the child.

For the Baby's Christmas morning,
When the Yuletide logs were burning,
Christmas presents from afar,
Laid beneath the Christmas star.
The baby rocked in his fireside bed.
Closed his eyes,
Nodded his head.

CHRISTMAS WITH THE RURAL MAIL
Author: Lance Woolaver
Artist: Maud Lewis

© 1979 Woolaver, Lance

ISBN 0-920852-04-1

Published by

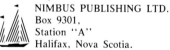 NIMBUS PUBLISHING LTD.
Box 9301,
Station "A"
Halifax, Nova Scotia.